SWAT
Secret World Adventure Team

Sent to
Sydney

by
Lisa Thompson

illustrated by
Stan Squire

PICTURE WINDOW BOOKS
Minneapolis, Minnesota

Editor: Jill Kalz
Page Production: Tracy Kaehler
Creative Director: Keith Griffin
Editorial Director: Carol Jones

First American edition published in 2006 by
Picture Window Books
5115 Excelsior Boulevard
Suite 232
Minneapolis, MN 55416
877-845-8392
www.picturewindowbooks.com

First published in Australia by
Blake Education Pty Ltd
CAN 074 266 023
Locked Bag 2022
Glebe NSW 2037
Ph: (02) 9518 4222; Fax: (02) 9518 4333
Email: mail@blake.com.au
www.askblake.com.au
© Blake Publishing Pty Ltd Australia 2005

Printed in the United States of America.

Library of Congress Cataloging-in-Publication Data
Thompson, Lisa, 1969-
Sent to Sydney / by Lisa Thompson ; illustrated by
Stan Squire.
p. cm. — (Read-it! chapter books. SWAT)
Summary: Dom and Ella enjoy some of the sights and sounds
of Sydney, Australia, while on a mission for the Secret
World Adventure Team one New Year's Eve.
ISBN 1-4048-1671-2 (hardcover)
[1. Adventure and adventurers—Fiction. 2. New Year—Fiction.
3. Sydney (N.S.W.)—Fiction. 4. Australia—Fiction.] I. Squire,
Stan, ill. II. Title. III. Series.
PZ7.T371634Sen 2005
[E]—dc22   2005027167

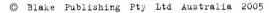

Table of Contents

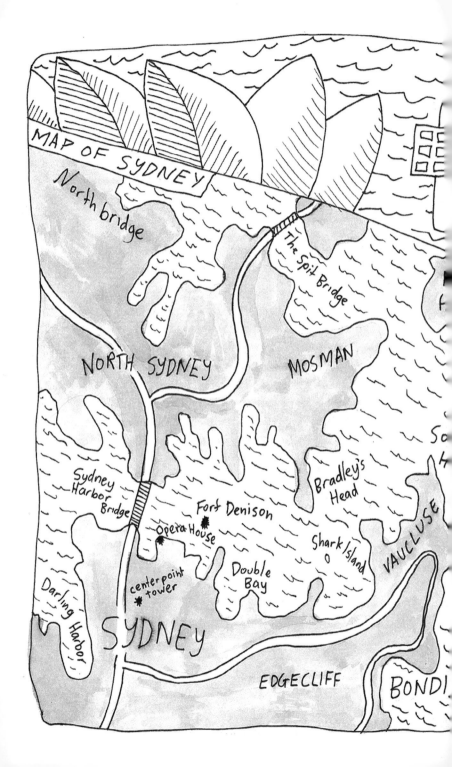

MAP OF SYDNEY

North bridge

The Spit Bridge

NORTH SYDNEY

MOSMAN

Sydney Harbor Bridge

Fort Denison

Bradley's Head

Opera House

Shark Island

VAUCLUSE

Darling Harbor

center point tower

Double Bay

SYDNEY

EDGECLIFF

BONDI

SWAT

DESTINATION PROFILE

DESTINATION ....Sydney, Australia...

POPULATION ...About 4 million...

LANGUAGE ...English...

MAJOR LANDMARKS ...Opera House

Harbor Bridge ...Centerpoint Tower

Hottest Month ...January...

coldest month ...July...

SWAT

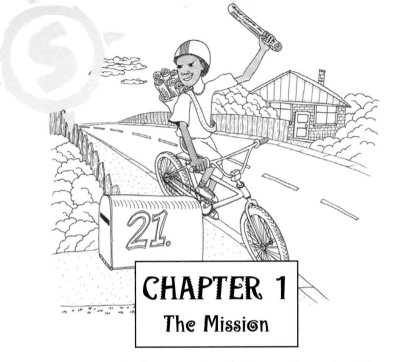

CHAPTER 1
The Mission

Dom sped down the hill on his BMX bike and turned tightly around the corner. He grabbed the newspaper in his left hand, lifted it high above his head, and threw it with everything he had. WACK! It hit the front step.

"Perfect shot!" he cried.

Dom rode into Wave Street and threw his last three papers. WACK! WACK! WACK! Three perfect shots in a row. It was time to head home.

As Dom walked in the front door, he burst out laughing.

"Nice outfit, Dad!"

"I'm wearing it to the New Year's Eve party tonight," his dad said.

Dom thought people acted really weird on the last day of the year. It was New Year's Eve, and people seemed to use this day as an excuse to do all kinds of silly stuff before the new year began.

"This is definitely going to be one of those weird days," said Dom, as he rode down to the bike track.

Dom loved riding at the BMX track. It was packed with cool jumps. When Dom arrived, his friend Ella was already waiting for him.

"How's it going, Dom?" she asked.

"Weird. I'm telling you, Ella, this is the one day of the year when anything can happen," Dom said.

"Tell me about it!" said Ella. "When I arrived, this package was sitting here. It's got our names on it. I've been waiting for you so we can open it."

Ella showed Dom the package. Sure enough, it read:

ATTENTION Ella and Dom

Dom looked around the track. There was no one else around.

Ella pulled at the package. "Hurry up, Dom! Let's open it. I'm dying to know what's inside!"

They tore open the package and found a portable CD player with a note. The note read:

Top Secret!
Hello, Dom and Ella.
This is a message from SWAT.
Please press **PLAY.**

Dom put on a headset, handed the other one to Ella, and pressed **PLAY**. At first, there was a faint, crackly sound, then a voice:

"Welcome, Dom and Ella. My name is Gosic. I am the voice of SWAT, which stands for Secret World Adventure Team. Congratulations! We have chosen you two for our next mission.

"We urgently need you in Sydney, Australia. Your mission will begin at Bondi Beach, where you will meet a boy named Jason. He will be riding a red bike.

"In this package you will find two SWAT transporter wristbands. You must wear these wristbands at all times. They will allow you to travel in the blink of an eye. Please leave at once! Good luck,. SWAT."

Dom and Ella slid on the wristbands, not really believing what was about to happen. They clicked the **START MISSION** button, just as the instructions said.

"Three. Two. One," they said.

Click.

START MISSION.

CHAPTER 2
Bondi Beach

Dom and Ella opened their eyes. They found themselves sitting on their bikes in the middle of the Bondi Beach car park.

"No way!" gasped Dom. He tapped his wristband. "These things really work. We're in Sydney!"

Ella rode a few circles on her bike to take in the view. She was about to jump the curb when she heard the honking of a car horn.

"Hey! Move your bike!" yelled a girl. Her car was loaded with surfboards.

"Sorry," said Ella, as she rode out of the way.

Dom looked out at the horizon. He shaded his eyes and squinted. Even though it was early, the sun was high, and the sky was cloudless and clear.

"Look at this beach! It's going to be one hot summer day," he said.

The parking lot and the beach were filling up quickly. People were swimming, and the lifeguards were already on patrol.

As Dom and Ella rode their bikes along the walkway, they noticed a tent outside the surf club. It was roped off, and a sign said, "Official Race Competitors Only."

OFFICIAL RACE
COMPETITORS ONLY

They tried to sneak through but were stopped right away.

"Are you kids competitors?" asked a large, musclebound man.

"Competitors for what?" asked Dom.

"The Surf Club Ironman race," the large man said.

"Ah, no, not exactly," mumbled Ella.

"Well, I'm sorry, but it's competitors only beyond this point," the man said.

Dom and Ella rode around the tent and beyond the surf club toward the far end of Bondi Beach.

"So, what's an Ironman race?" Ella asked Dom.

"It's a race filled with lots of activities. Competitors swim, board paddle, surf, and run, all in one long race. You really have to be super-fit. Are you thinking about entering?" Dom teased.

"No!" cried Ella.

"I want to find Jason, like the message said. Let's get going," said Dom.

Cars streamed down Bondi Hill and cruised down the main street. People headed for the sand and for the rows of cafes and shops that overlooked the water. Backpackers walked up and down, looking for a place to stay. Competitors were arriving and setting up their gear. Surfers headed for the surf, and skaters headed for the skate ramp. Groups of girls lay on the grass eating french fries covered in ketchup. They had to fight off the seagulls, all hungry for a fry.

People from all over the world were at Bondi Beach. Ella heard accents from everywhere: Great Britain, Ireland, Italy, Greece, Israel, Japan, and New Zealand.

"There are people from everywhere here. How are we ever going to find this Jason guy?" asked Ella.

Dom didn't answer. He was too busy watching the surf. The swell from the south was creating good waves at the northern end. The sun shone through the face of the waves as they peeled down the beach.

As the surf rolled into the shore, Dom watched the surfers paddle for a wave. First they'd jostle for position, then paddle until the wave had them. With a quick jump to their feet, the surfers would glide down the waves.

"Awesome. I'd love to be able to do that," said Dom, as he watched a surfer ride a wave, turn, and paddle out to catch another.

CHAPTER 3
Jason

"I think that's Jason!" Ella pointed to a guy trying to fix a red bike.

"It looks like he's got some major problems," said Dom.

"Hi! Need a hand?" asked Ella, riding up to him. "I'm Ella, and this is my friend Dom."

"Hi, I'm Jason. I just broke a sprocket, and I wrecked the front wheel. Now I'm never going to finish my job and be ready for the race."

"Are you entering the Ironman race?" asked Dom.

"I was going to," Jason said. "I have to deliver some CDs first, and then I was going to come back and race. I don't know anyone else who can get the job done in time."

Dom rode off up the hill, turned, and sped back down.

"What's he doing?" asked Jason.

Dom jumped the curb and sped through the parked cars. He flipped a wheelie and then came to a halt right in front of them.

Jason was impressed. "That was awesome riding!" he said.

"Excellent thinking, SWAT agent," whispered Ella.

"Maybe you two could deliver the CDs for me. Would you? Ride like that, and you'll be there in no time," Jason said.

Dom's plan had worked. Jason gave his pack to Ella and explained the job.

"I'm supposed to deliver these CDs to a bunch of technical people around the city. There's a laser show over Sydney Harbor tonight for New Year's Eve. You need to take one CD to each address. Have someone at each place sign this form, and make sure all of the CDs are delivered before 4 P.M."

"What if they're not?" asked Ella,
looking over the map of Sydney.

"Then the whole population of Sydney,
almost four million people, will blame
YOU for wrecking the New Year's Eve
laser show," said Jason.

Jason laughed, but somehow Dom
and Ella could tell it wasn't really a
laughing matter. Jason looked back at
the beach. Ella and Dom could see
how important this race was to him.

"We'll deliver the CDs. Don't worry about that. We'll meet you back here this afternoon," said Dom.

"Be here by 4:30 P.M.," said Jason. "Then you'll be able to watch me cross the finish line."

"Deal. See you at 4:30," said Dom.

Jason took off to get ready. "Thanks a ton, guys! See you later."

CHAPTER 4
Shark Island

"I say we use our transporter wristbands to get to these places. That way, we'll be finished in no time and might even be able to go for a swim," said Ella.

While Dom chained their bikes to a rack, Ella scanned the list of places where the CDs had to be delivered.

"Where to first?" asked Dom.

"Shark Island," said Ella as calmly as she could.

"What?" Dom's hair stood on end.

"Calm down," laughed Ella. "It's called that because it's shaped like a shark."

"Phew! You had me worried there for a minute! In that case, let's start the countdown. Three. Two. One."

Click.

"Ouch! Get me out of here. I've landed in a prickle bush!" Dom's feet were up in the air, and his body was wrapped in the bush.

Ella did her best to get him out, but he wouldn't stop moving.

"Hold still, you're only making it worse!" she cried.

Dom emerged from the bush and checked out the island.

"This island is in the middle of Sydney Harbor," he said. "How was Jason going to deliver a CD here?" Dom scanned the shore.

"Look! I think that's the guy we're looking for." Ella pointed to a man sitting cross-legged on a rock by the water. Next to him was the tower that housed the laser light machine. The man sat perfectly still. "What do you think he's doing?"

"No idea. Probably just sitting there thinking up some wacky New Year's Eve stuff for later," said Dom.

As they moved closer, they noticed a group of pelicans. They took another step. The branches and twigs under their feet cracked loudly. The pelicans were startled and flew away.

The man turned around. "Are you here to deliver the CD?" he asked.

Dom held out the form. "Would you sign here, please?"

The man stood up.

"Why were you sitting like that on the rock?" asked Ella.

"If you're perfectly still, the animals will come right up to you and won't be afraid. Sometimes the birds come, sometimes the possums. You should try it and see what happens." He turned and began to climb the laser tower.

Dom wriggled and jumped around.

"Well, no animal is going to come near us with you jumping up and down like that!" scolded Ella.

"It's the prickles!" cried Dom. "I'm itchy all over." He lifted his shirt and showed Ella his spotty rash.

"Try not to think about it. Distract yourself," Ella said, as she ripped a young leaf from a eucalyptus tree. "I saw someone play a eucalyptus leaf on TV. If you blow on it, it buzzes."

Dom tried. "BZZZZZZZZZZZZZ."

"Great job, Dom! You just sprayed me!"
Ella was not impressed.

"Come on," said Dom. "We're off to
the city, Centerpoint Tower to be exact.
Three. Two. One."

Click.

CHAPTER 5
A Bird's Eye View

In the blink of an eye, Dom and Ella found themselves standing high above Sydney on the observation deck of Centerpoint Tower. They walked around its circular room. Sydney stretched as far as the eye could see.

To the north, they watched the ferries heading to Manly. To the east, they saw cargo ships entering Sydney Harbor. To the west, the blue haze of the Blue Mountains hovered, and to the south, the green of the Royal National Park glowed. Below them lay the busy city streets.

"Let's put some money in the binoculars so we can see better," said Dom.

People rushed in and out of offices and shops and ran to catch buses and trains. Ella didn't like standing so close to the window. Looking down made her feel a little sick.

"I can see the fountain in Hyde Park, and the Opera House, and there are some people fishing off the point in the Botanic Gardens," Dom said.

Dom was moving the binoculars around so much that Ella wondered how he could see anything at all!

"Dom, I'm going to look for the next laser person," Ella said.

It didn't take Ella long to find him. He was wearing the same overalls as the man on Shark Island. Ella handed him the CD, and he signed the form.

Ella looked down through the huge windows and watched the people on the streets. They all look like ants, she thought.

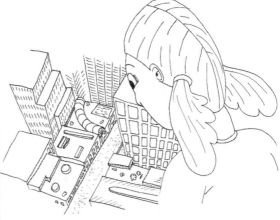

"Ella, Ella!" Dom ran toward her excitedly. "I watched this video about the tower, about how they made it and stuff. Did you know that in high winds the tower sways? And the long column that this observation deck sits on is really an elevator shaft. The elevators go up and down really, really fast. Let's go down the elevator. It'll be tons of fun."

Dom dragged Ella toward the elevator and said, "There are 1,370 steps up the tower, Ella, and this guy, he holds the record for being the fastest man to climb them. It took him just seven minutes and 29 seconds! Can you believe that?"

Ella and Dom got into the elevator and sped down.

"WHHOOOOOOEEE! My insides!" said Ella, as she held her stomach.

"Excellent," said Dom. "How cool did that feel? It makes your stomach drop."

Dom loved it. Ella looked a little sick.

"Let's go!" she said. "The next drop-off point is Sydney Harbor Bridge."

00217 007 00·04·02 09:55

Albert Ave. Car Park
KEEP YOUR TICKET WITH YOU

ENTRY SUBJECT
TO CONDITIONS OF
ENTRY DISPLAYED
AT THE ENTRANCE
TO AND IN THE

CARPARK HOURS:
Monday - Saturday
8am - 1am

CHAPTER 6
The Harbor Bridge

The big gray bridge stretched across the harbor like a giant coat hanger.

"Are you here for the tour?" asked a woman standing next to one of the pylons. "Great! Well, let's go. We haven't got all day."

"We're actually ...," Ella said. She tried to interrupt the woman, but it was hopeless.

"Please put these harnesses on, and we'll begin the climb," the woman said. "Make sure you connect the harness to the handrail, otherwise you could fall off." She let out a little laugh.

Ella and Dom looked over the side and down. They didn't find it funny. It was a very long way down into the harbor.

The tour woman kept talking. "This bridge links the northern and southern parts of the city. It opened on March 19, 1932, and it is the largest bridge in Australia. There are six million rivets and more than 58,000 tons (52,200 metric tons) of steel. About 150,000 vehicles cross it everyday," she said.

"It takes 10 years to paint the whole bridge," she continued. "So, as soon as the painters finish, they have to start all over again."

On and on the woman talked as they climbed. Then, finally, she stopped and drew a breath. "Here we are, ladies and gentlemen! The best view in town."

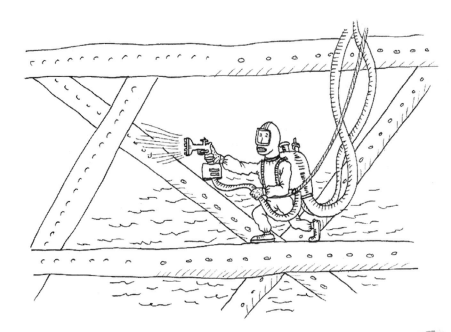

Ella and Dom looked up. They were at the very top of the Sydney Harbor Bridge! The view was awesome. Ella forgot all about her fear of heights.

Dom held out his arms. "I feel like I'm flying!" he cried.

It was cold and windy up so high. They stayed for a while, taking in the view and watching the boats in the harbor.

They almost forgot why they were there, until the tour woman said, "Don't mind the technician here. He's preparing for the laser show tonight."

"Excellent!" said Ella. "Just the person we've been looking for."

55

Dom handed the man the CD and the form to sign. Then Dom and Ella started the walk back down the bridge.

When they reached solid ground, Ella lay flat on the grass. "That view was cool, but I really love being back on the ground."

"Well, don't get too comfortable," said Dom. "We've got one more CD to deliver, and we have to go there now." He pointed to a little fort in the middle of the harbor. "Fort Denison!" he announced. "Three. Two. One."

Click.

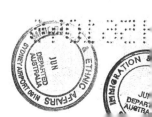

CHAPTER 7
The Last CD

"Stand by to turn!" yelled the captain.
"Pull on that line! Haul in the jib! Let
out the mainsail! Hurry up! Faster!
Faster! We don't have all day! Let's get
that spinnaker up. Not like that, you'll
jam the winch. Come here, girl." He
beckoned to Ella. "Take over the helm
while I sort out this mess."

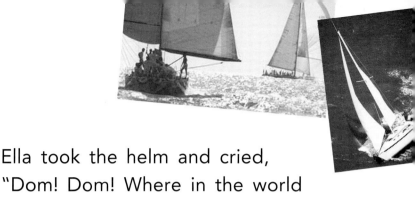

Ella took the helm and cried, "Dom! Dom! Where in the world are we?"

"There's Fort Denison!" Dom shouted. "We must have missed it and ended up on a yacht. Ella, we're racing!"

As he said that, the mainsail and spinnaker filled with air. The yacht shot across the water, heading toward the Opera House.

"We don't have time for this!" cried Ella. "We have to deliver the last CD. Do something, Dom!"

The captain took over the helm again.

"Now's our chance!" cried Dom. He grabbed a life raft and threw it overboard. He climbed in and held it steady. "Quick, Ella, jump!"

As soon as Ella hit the raft, she looked behind her. The yacht had gained speed and was moving away quickly.

"Fort Denison's over there," cried Dom.

The little raft bobbed up and down in the water. Ella and Dom paddled as hard as they could.

"Faster, Ella!" Dom yelled. "It's 3:40 already. We don't have a lot of time."

Their arms ached as they paddled hard to the pier. Time was running out.

To get off, they needed to lasso the pier. Dom lifted the rope in his left hand, the same hand he used to deliver newspapers. Ella tried to keep the boat steady. Dom gave it his best shot.

"Perfect," cried Ella.

Dom pulled them to the pier, and they climbed ashore.

"We only have 10 minutes left," said Ella. "We've got to find the person to give this CD to."

"That must be me," said the woman in the doorway of the fort. "I saw you two as you jumped off the yacht. That was very impressive."

Dom handed over the CD, and the woman signed the form.

"Well, I'd better get started," she said. "You made it just in time. This laser show is going to be sensational. Where are you going to watch it from?"

Dom looked at Ella. "We hadn't even thought about that."

"I recommend Bradley's Head," she said, pointing to the other side of the harbor. "You'll get a spectacular view from there."

CHAPTER 8
Jason's Race

By the time Dom and Ella got back to Bondi Beach, the Ironman race was almost over. In the final leg of the race, competitors had to ride the rescue board through the surf and then run up the beach to the finish line.

Spectators lined the beach to watch. The competitors had already rounded the last buoy.

Jason was neck and neck with another man. A wave came, and they both caught it, riding into the shore. Jason ran quickly out of the water and threw his board down. He and his opponent hit the sand together and ran for the finish line.

"Go, Jason! Go!" yelled Dom and Ella.

With his last bit of energy, Jason threw himself over the finish line. The crowd cheered loudly.

Ella and Dom ran to congratulate him. "You won! You won! Way to go! Congratulations, Jason!"

"Thanks, guys," Jason panted, his chest heaving. "I couldn't have won if you hadn't helped me out!"

People crowded around and lifted Jason onto the podium. Ella and Dom felt their wristbands vibrate. A message appeared on the screen:

Well done, SWAT! Mission successful.

A red button appeared marked **MISSION RETURN.**

Jason returned with his medal and three surfboards.

"I hope you're ready," said Jason. "We're all going surfing!"

Jason gave them a quick lesson on the sand. Then they ran into the water for the real thing.

Ella and Dom sat on their boards and looked at the beach. A breeze started to blow.

"This has been the strangest and coolest New Year's Eve ever!" said Dom. "I knew it was going to be a weird day, but I didn't think it was going to be anything like this."

"You're going to get clobbered!" yelled Ella, looking at the size of the wave coming toward them.

"AHHHHHHHHH!" Dom flew down the giant wave.

"SWAT agent Ella to the rescue," Ella laughed. "Three. Two. One."

Click.

MISSION RETURN.

GLOSSARY

backpackers—people who travel cheaply and take only what they can fit in their backpacks

buoy—a floating device to mark the course of a race

eucalyptus tree—a kind of tree native to Australia

harness—a safety belt or strap

helm—the device for steering a yacht

jib—the small sail on a yacht

jostle—to push and shove

mainsail—the large sail on a yacht

Opera House—a theater at Sydney Harbor, famous for its unusual shape

podium—a small platform

pylons—tall structures at the entrance to a bridge

spinnaker—a large sail on a yacht, used only when sailing with the wind

sprocket—the part of a bicycle that holds and moves the chain

squint—to look through partly closed eyes

technician—a person skilled in a technical area

winch—a handle used to wind up a sail

SWAT

IT COULD BE YOU!

Secret World Adventure Team

COME TRAVEL TODAY!

A complete list of *Read-it!* Chapter Books is
available on our Web site:
www.picturewindowbooks.com